SAUDADE

NO LONGER PROPERTY OF
SEATTLE PUBLIC LIBRARY

SAUDADE

Suneeta Peres da Costa

**TRANSIT
BOOKS**

Published by Transit Books
2301 Telegraph Avenue, Oakland, California 94612
www.transitbooks.org

First published in Australia by Giramondo Publishing, 2018
Copyright © Suneeta Peres da Costa 2018

FIRST US EDITION 2019
LIBRARY OF CONGRESS CONTROL NUMBER: 2019946299

DESIGN & TYPESETTING
Justin Carder

DISTRIBUTED BY
Consortium Book Sales & Distribution
(800) 283-3572 | cbsd.com

Printed in the United States of America

9 8 7 6 5 4 3 2 1

All rights reserved. This book or any portion thereof may not be reproduced or used in any manner whatsoever without the express written permission of the publisher except for the use of brief quotations in a book review.

For Mridula Nath Chakraborty

The imagination is always united with a desire, that is to say a value. Only desire without an object is empty of imagination. There is the real presence of God in everything which imagination does not veil. The beautiful takes our desire captive and empties it of its object, giving it an object which is present and thus forbidding it to fly off towards the future.

—Simone Weil, *Gravity and Grace*

SAUDADE

1

My mother told me that the dead walk backward; she said, they try to walk forward but can only walk backward. When she told me that, I was sitting on the step that led from the kitchen to the compound, my hand cupped on her kneecap. A draught of shadows from the pink guava tree splayed on the concrete when the sunlight pierced the clouds overhead. That was our first house, the one in which I was born in Benguela, and I can still see it in my mind's eye, close and shimmering like a still life, although it probably has like so much else now gone…She had asked Caetano to fetch a papaya for our breakfast and while we waited for him we watched the guinea cock that my father had brought home as a gift from a client in Uíge: it did not crow, did not make a sound, only silently circled the compound, opening and shutting the tiny aperture of its beak, pecking uselessly for seed. When I clapped my hands, it did not scamper in fright, only bristled its red comb and lifted its tired wings. My mother said that if I dreamt of someone with their feet about-facing I should be sure to shout to wake myself up, because the nearer they seemed, the further they would have led me to their world, the world of the dead. I turned to face her: it was just then my favourite occupation simply to watch her. Her beautiful eyes, outlined with *kohl*, grew large and small, accentuating by turns this part of what she said, now that. It was the middle of the dry season but each time her lips parted I found myself in an oasis in which I wanted for nothing; I had no need to look at the horizon but if I did, it would have gone on and on, a hungerlessness that might well be called paradise. The wind was blowing from the coast, a salt wind from the Atlantic which I would feel against me as a phantom presence even when it was not there any more. The sun was not shining and its not shining was neither here nor there; I was not waiting for the sun to reveal itself to me…Although I was old enough – three years old, perhaps four – I seldom spoke at this time. No one really remarked on this fact nor how I hung off every one of my mother's words. Indeed, I could have continued in this same vein for an aeon or more, unaware of the peril of what might lie ahead. That her words could come to have a dangerous sway over me – that they might make me look this way and that, only in vain, only to be met by a darkness which was also unnameable – I could not have conceived, for I was more contented by the fact of her voice than what she had to say. At that time, there were so many things I did not know; my mind and body were like a *tabula rasa* on which much would be written, even if later I might want it all to be erased too…She said that *bruxas*, being consorts of the dead, have twisted feet. Soon Caetano returned; he was carrying the papaya under one arm and a tin of honey in his other hand; it was quite a balancing act and yet he was able to secure the papaya under his arm as though it were second nature to him. Caetano wore an old pair of my father's shoes; they were a little too big and so it seemed he might trip over at any moment. That morning Papá had joked that if Caetano were to die we would have to bury him in these shoes. My father had made this quip in Konkani. When he was angry, or trying to be funny, Papá spoke in Konkani. I did not yet know that Konkani was a tongue that might have belonged to a people from whom I was also descended, to a place and time of which I nevertheless had no memory, and so it was neither discordant nor alluring to my ear. My mother moved fluently between Portuguese and Konkani and the tone she used with me or my father no different than that she used to speak to Ifigênia and Caetano. She took the old tin when Caetano held it out to her, winked and said, At this rate we could go into business. She turned the few honeycombs that lay at the bottom of the tin towards the light and said, What do you say, Caetano? Caetano smiled uneasily, shrugged and made to brush something away from his face. His hair in that light was a copper colour. His father was a Dane who had settled on a coffee plantation in Mozambique only to return to Copenhagen when he had grown tired of the East African plains; his mother, a native of Cabo Delgado, had died when he was small so he had been brought up in a Lourenço Marques orphanage. Now when his hair fell over his eyes, my mother said he ought to get a haircut. Yes, Mummy, Caetano answered, swatting an invisible fly before his face. It was curious to hear him call her Mummy; he was still a child when he had come to my parents, some years before I was born, and now he might have been thirteen or fourteen and full of a wary self-consciousness. When he shifted his weight from one foot to another, my mother sighed and passed the papaya into my own small arms. Its skin was green speckled black; it felt cool and heavy and I wondered what would happen if it fell, what sound it would make when it hit the ground, whether it would split or roll away…She disappeared into the kitchen and appeared again with a few hundred centavos that she dropped into Caetano's hand. He put the change into his pocket and passed quickly through the garden. My mother followed him to the gate. On either side the road was long and empty: a woman was returning from the dyeing factory, a child slung on her back; a fisherman clutching a small bundle of leftover catch walked by. My mother led me inside again, but only a few steps on stopped to look back; she looked back, clicked her tongue and said that there was no race like the Bantu race that had to be cosseted like a child because it could not look after itself. What a tragedy, she said, to be a person who cannot take care of his own affairs, who never grows up, for that is the fate not only of the blacks of Angola but all black Africans! If it surprised me to hear her talk this way, it was not a great devastation. If her eyes and mouth were not the reassuring shapes that they had been a moment before, I did not yet have cause to identify with the confused souls of Babel. Now she set about making breakfast. She peeled the papaya and cut it into long canoes, the way I liked it. As always, she boiled the milk, removing the skin with a spoon and swallowing it before setting the glass before me. She allowed me a mouthful of the honey before bottling it and storing it in the larder. The moist, unmoving eyes of the mackerel gleamed from the marble cutting board. Ifigênia was grinding the coconut and chillies for the *recheado* and, as she wandered down the corridor to give her an instruction, I watched my mother's legs: she was wearing a house dress of beige linen; she had not put on her knee-highs and so her legs were bare. Her legs were bare but they did not look vulnerable; they were as strong and dependable as the trunk of any one of the trees that rose in the small orchard beyond the compound – I could see the tips of the branches through the open door: guava, lime and papaya. Her feet appeared to blossom out of her legs, and were so pretty that I could not imagine her being dead, I could not imagine it, though the thought would not leave me and I felt I had to keep looking each few minutes from her face to her toes to confirm that they were pointing in the same direction.

2

THE BRAZILIAN MUTINEERS from the Santa Maria did not get to the harbour of Luanda. Captain Galvão did not start a revolution. None of the prisoners that escaped from the São Paulo penitentiary tapped on our door, entreating us to harbour him as a fugitive. Yet in the days after the revolt at Baixa de Cassanje, there was a telex to say that a client of Papá's, a German cotton-farm owner, had been killed in a northern reprisal. As he got ready to attend the funeral, my father spoke in a low voice about the circumstances of this man's murder. My mother was in the kitchen, standing by the open door and I was playing just outside, turning the large, asymmetrical ears of Crio inside out, watching them flop back when he got bothered with the flies...Each time Papá said the word murder, my mother raised her eyebrows, glanced my way and then off toward the garden. I tried to picture the dead cotton-farm owner in his coffin – bound in tourniquets like the Egyptian mummies I had glimpsed in an old copy of *National Geographic* — in a simple robe like Jesus in the Passion. I wondered if it was because he was a stranger that it was so difficult to imagine him dead. When Papá went to the funeral I imagined what would happen if I could not recognise the cotton-farm owner when he appeared to make his fatal overture. Dona Angela paid us a visit. She had come from Madeira with her husband and they had started a business selling dry goods in the centre of Benguela. But her husband had died suddenly – a heart attack. That was only the beginning of her troubles, for soon the money evaporated and debts began to mount. She was homesick, my mother had told me, and that accounted for her nervous temperament. Homesick for what, I wondered, for where? Ifigênia had just fried some *papos de anjos* and my mother asked her to set them on the table. I sat by her, watching Dona Angela blowing cool air on her tea and absentmindedly devouring one after the other until the *papos*, slightly scorched, had vanished. When Ifigênia had left, Dona Angela lowered her voice and said she was afraid to go to sleep at night. She said, We gave education, housing and hospitals to the blacks – where would they be without us? I looked at that moment from Dona Angela's face to my mother's: my mother's face was calm and serene. It was as though the sun was shining where she was; she seemed to be at once aware of what Dona Angela was saying and yet quite indifferent to it. She nodded, telling Dona Angela that she was quite right to be upset but meanwhile she was observing the plumes of smoke issuing from the bee boxes where Caetano was busy checking on the hives. I turned again to Dona Angela: her large body was cloaked in a heavy mantle of mourning; her hair was limp and thin; her brow was furrowed and a morsel of custard sat unflatteringly on her thick, lower lip. Perhaps she had been a young and pretty woman when she first came from Portugal, but now her face was ravaged – not only from the extraordinary misfortune of losing her husband but besieged by terror about an uncertain future, and all her gestures seemed colonised by this fear…Putting two

fingers to her pulse, she said she felt faint and coughed to dem-
onstrate her catarrh. My mother asked her if she had been to
see her specialist and she answered that the doctors in Benguela were all charlatans and that she would not let them near
her for her life. Dona Angela then began to reminisce about
her son Mathias, and the loving letters he wrote her from Lisbon; she said it was her heart's delight to receive these letters,
what a boon it was to have a son, she said, for daughters were
no guarantee…against what she did not say. When my eyes
crossed the network of varicose veins to Dona Angela's feet,
I noticed she had no ankles to speak of. It was as though a bee
had stung her, her ankles were so swollen. It must have per-
turbed me to look at these legs without joints which burgeoned
into her feet because I remember looking away and again at
her ankles. She caught me and told me I was getting shifty. She
said, Sly or shy I'm not sure which but a child should speak
when she is spoken to! To her surprise, and that of my mother,
I then loudly enunciated that I would soon be going to school…
When Dona Angela left my mother stood for some time in the
front room. Daylight streamed onto the array of family por-
traits, distant strangers with dark skin like my own, dressed up
in dresses and suits like good women and men of the Empire.
My mother turned to me but as she opened her mouth it
seemed she began haranguing these mute portraits. She said
that Dona Angela had gall; she said everyone knew that her
son Mathias was not studying accountancy at all but living a
dissipated life in Lisbon and only wrote to finagle money she
didn't have. She said there was never a clearer case for a dandy
and that all gays were mama's boys…I trailed my mother
through the house, at every corner imagining the dead cotton-

farm owner appearing on backward-facing feet, rounding on us with a scythe lodged in his breast. She told me to come nap with her but the mosquitoes, humming in the dusky air, kept me awake, so I wandered onto the front porch where it was cooler, waiting for some deathly footsteps, but only the postboy came, whistling a Cape Verdean folk song; it must have been a *morna* of Eugénio Tavares. When he lifted the catch to put the letters in the box he looked up, saw me and laughed. Admittedly I must have been an odd sight: my hair wet with sweat; my mouth agape. He then started to say something; I could not understand what he was saying because he spoke in Creole. I did not imagine that he was giving voice to a private thought, derisive or mocking, one that he in any case did not care to share with me; I was happy to hear him speaking, to hear this other voice with its unusual cadences...My mother appeared and, when he saw her, the postboy stopped what he was saying in mid-sentence and started down the street. When he was out of earshot, she said that she was sure the postboy was a communist and that I was not to speak to him again. I had no idea what a communist was, but I assumed that it must be something malevolent, something like the dead. The sky grew dark. The rains had ended but still it seemed there would be a downpour. Sitting on the cane chair, I could feel the mosquitoes at my legs, their tender stinging sensations at the extremities of my toes. In the distance I could hear the braking of the freight trains along the Benguela railway, the machinery of the Diamang mine, the droning of crude oil generators...One of Ifigênia's friends, Philomena, whom she called Memu, came by; I could hear them talking in lowered voices in Kimbundu. Ifigênia had been told to speak Portuguese in my company but she often forgot and spoke Kimbundu anyway. Though I could understand only a smattering, I found Kimbundu, with its spirited rhythms, beautiful. And if it did not occur to me that they may have been talking about me, this was less because of humility than because it had not yet dawned on me that Kimbundu might be the language, as I might be the source, of some of their plaints and grievances. When this became evident I might find Kimbundu a cacophony, at the first sound of which I would reach for pliable beeswax to stop up my ears! I found my way into the compound and opened the coop. A hen had been bought to companion the cock, but one morning, finding her bloody and near-dead from his rapacious love-making, Papá had taken the cock to be destroyed. The hen had hatched chicks but bore them no love and now wobbled about with a furious and deranged look in her black eyes, her plumage of white feathers turned tawny and grey. Now when I imagined the dead man, the image I conjured was of a figure tall of stature and with a heavy step, moustachioed and precious about his appearance. Indeed, this description may have applied just as easily to my father and, in anticipating the footfall of the dead man, I was also anticipating the footfall of Papá. I was so accustomed to his footsteps coming and going, and now I wondered what would happen if we didn't hear his approach at all? It was just then he turned into the drive. As he stepped out of the car, he was ashen-faced and I could see he was perspiring heavily under the black hat he had ceremoniously worn. He pulled me up, dusted my dress and admonished me it was not good for the servants to see me sitting in the dirt like that. Do you know whose daughter you are? he asked me with sudden ferocity. His breath, tobacco mixed with whiskey, was pungent and I wriggled like a chick out of his arms. He chased the tattered hen which fled in his wake and shut her back in the coop. Caetano was smoking nearby and Papá muttered to him about leaving the coop open. Caetano had lately developed the habit of looking through Papá and now, as I followed my father inside, I felt Caetano looking through me too. That night, I could not go to sleep easily because I imagined meeting the dead in my dreams. I stayed awake for a long time, waiting for the dead cotton-farm owner's appearance. During the night I woke my mother and she told me not to stir. She said that as long as she slept beside me nothing could happen, that if she saw me being led away by someone from the dead world she would call my name, and when she called my name I would come to her at once.

3

ONE EVENING DURING THE RAINS my parents began to get ready to go to a party in Luanda. They were to stay overnight in a hotel because it would be over quite late and the roads back to Benguela would be difficult to see. It was an important party; if it turned out all right Papá would be promoted and we would be posted to Luanda. He was a labour lawyer, working for the Ministry of the Interior, preparing workers' contracts…I was too young to have understood the liabilities he dealt with were human: that the men and women against whose sicknesses and accidents he insured Portuguese and other European pastoralists were native contract labourers. It did not occur to me then that, to protect the interests of the owner of an iron-ore mine against his labourers' lung disease, tuberculosis and cataracts, a person may become blind after his own fashion; or that to insure a maize farmer against the hookworm suffered by his indentured workers, one might begin to feel a kind of parasite. That these workers, bought and sold as the slaves had once been, often died from exhaustion in the course of their bonded labour, is something of which I understood the implications only later; when everything shattered, I glimpsed it clearly, albeit through the shards of memory. I came to see how the past, like some ancient *karma*, inscribes itself on the body as much as the mind, so that what we do to others returns to haunt us in the subtlest manner. Although his body was not broken by the weight of a felled plane tree, or deafened by a harvester, Papá was in his own way sickened by so many secrets he was keeping, and we were increasingly hostage to his moods, to his silences and sudden outbursts, his sudden demonstrations of affection and withdrawal. He was in his study, his back turned – a boulder I would so many times liked to have rolled away. Behind that boulder, he might have been pouring whiskey into a glass or poring over some papers. Although I was forbidden to play there, it was a perfect temptation and when he was not home I would not be able to resist the urge to try out his rotational chair, imagining myself the important owner of his fountain pen, his Definitivos, the ivory letter opener. In the bottommost locked drawer I knew there was a carbine pistol which his boss, Senhor Mascarenhas, had given to him the previous year, on the anniversary of his employment…Now he turned to me, scowling slightly; his hair was slick with Brylcreem and as luminous as the patent leather of his brogues. In the bedroom, my mother was getting dressed, under her breath humming 'Manhã de Carnaval'. At first they had quarrelled because she wanted to stay in Benguela, but Papá had won her over with talk of a house with a bigger garden. She now told me if I were good and obeyed Ifigênia, she would bring back a treat from Luanda. I hoped it would be a doll I had seen in a shop window in the Rua de Camões, an American doll called Annie who gurgled when a cord was pulled in her back and whose blue eyes rolled about in her celluloid head. Through the window, I could see Caetano in the garden and in the distance Crio chasing a flock of turacos. I went back to colouring the pages of my book. The book told the story of the botanist Garcia de Orta and had all sorts of tropical flowers depicted in its pages, pink lotus, as well as the simples de Orta was famous for using medicinally, their names printed in italics beneath each picture. When these books had been given to us, during my first weeks at school, we had been asked to write our names inside the cover and I wrote mine with such a flourish that the teacher had singled me out for praise, displaying my handwriting as an example to the other children...How it had pleased me to bask in that praise, to be the favourite and the envy of my peers; I did not know my exalted status would not last nor that I would find infamy just as intoxicating. Now as I coloured the leaves and flowers, my mother pulled a *sari* from a neatly folded stack in her wardrobe. She unfolded it across the bed – mauve with small sprays of yellow blossoms like those on the pages of my book. It was the first time I had seen her wear a *sari*, and the way she wound it, as if with an intimate acquaintance of its pleats, about the light-green *chole*, was a revelation. She was humming, 'From the strings of my guitar, which sought only your love, arises a voice, because here comes the morning of Carnaval...', and I noticed that her bare feet only just emerged from the hemline of the long and manifold skirt. She then moved something and, as if from nowhere, found a *bindu*. She sifted briskly through her jewellery box. I knew this box was a wedding gift from her best friend Meeta's family in Goa. It was made of a carved timber; the carving was so artful as to make the two elephants that were on the lid appear to be braying in relief. My mother now pointed them out to me; she said these elephants were Indian elephants, not African ones, because the Indian elephant had smaller ears, she did not know why, most likely they had had a common ancestor, but some-where in their ancient genealogy they had developed differ-ently...As she fastened a pair of gold earrings to her lobes, I again took the opportunity to compare the reflection of her feet in the bureau mirror to her actual feet and, although I knew it was only a trick of the glass, I wondered what would happen if a dead person entered my dreams wearing a *sari* so long that I could not tell if their feet were turned backward or forward and what would happen if, having led me away, she were not there to call my name while I walked off into oblivion. When she stood away from her reflection and asked if she looked pretty, I could only stare at the lacuna where her feet had been. She clicked her tongue. She pointed to the reflection of my face in the bureau mirror and said that with my darker complexion I took after Papá's people. I knew who these were, or at least I knew they referred to the solemn faces of the por-traits hanging in the living room which I had come to study, their eyes if not their feet somehow following me. When she received news from them, my mother would open the thin blue aerogrammes, skim their contents then leave them on the kitchen table for my father. When she received aerogrammes from her own family or Meeta, she would take them onto the step of the compound to savour alongside a cup of spiced tea. All of these were kept in her bureau drawer with some coins and stamps commemorating Mahatma Gandhi and other leaders of the Independence, old glass bangles, and photo-graphs – including one of a handsome man I did not recognise in a military uniform...Now when she lifted the bottom of the *sari* above her knees, she removed a blood-soaked pad, being careful not to soil the fabric. When she replaced it, she looked up at me and said casually, matter-of-factly, Though in this respect you can be sure you'll take after me. She continued with her hair; she made a canopy of it and, after sweeping it up, subdued the ponytail into a coil which she pinned at the base of her scalp. She applied *kohl* to her eyes and a dark red lipstick to her lips. She took up the bottle of cologne and pressed the stopper to her wrists and behind her ears. The way she admired herself, it was as though she were performing a well-choreographed dance. I could sense she was not trying to impress me with this dance, was not really seeking my approval, but I wondered whose it might be she sought...My father suddenly emerged and asked did she want to make a spectacle wearing a *sari* among the people who might promote him in the Administration? He shouted, Change at once! The telephone rang and he lurched down the corridor to answer. He spoke in Konkani. There was a long silence before he called my mother to the phone. She doubled over and sobbed. Her mother had fallen gravely ill. There were few details, other than that, buying fish, she had fallen in the village market in Goa and been taken to a hospital where she had developed septicaemia. She was not expected to survive the next few days. I looked down at my picture of Garcia de Orta sporting his horn-rimmed spectacles and studying a blossom somewhere in the Ilha da Boa Vida; in various places, I had coloured outside the lines...Papá said he would not be able stay with us as Senhor Mascarenhas was expecting him. After all, he said, many important things depended on his going. My mother nodded stoically and I watched through the front window as he went quickly to the car. When he had gone, I followed my mother into the bedroom where she began removing her jewellery, her makeup and then slowly unwinding the *sari* so the costume that had just festooned the room fell away.

4

WHEN WE MOVED TO THE CAPITAL my mother resolved that we should make a new impression on the world too. Papá was often away on business and so Caetano drove – and as we passed from the new district into the old district of the city, I read the street names: Rua do Senado da Câmara; Rua de Dom João II; Rua de António Enes. I recited them to myself with wonder, as Galileo might have recited the relation of the earth to the sun and the planets rotating in their vast orbits: Avenida dos Combatentes da Grande Guerra; Rua do Coronel de Paiva. I did not know they were merely set out on the same grid as Lisbon, being a mirror of the colonial imaginary. And now that the names of the streets have changed, I wonder would I recognise them or be lost when moving through them again?...As I accompanied her on errands to the bank, to the hairdresser, to the market, my mother would tell me whom to greet, what to say, even how we should walk away. From the Rua de Camões we entered the Baixa and she found her way to merchants whose supplies she favoured. There was an officious Saudi who had the bags of fruit and citrus measured out exactly. We bought spices from a dealer from the Antilles; his prices were inflated, but the aroma of his cumin, peppercorns, turmeric and cloves was irresistible. We bought coffee and a particular kind of tobacco for Papá from a Guinean merchant who suffered a skin disease – my mother told me not to stare. From a garrulous old woman called Francesca who was said to have a lot of lovers we bought cassava flour and palm oil. Francesca's African grey parrot perched on her shoulder and greeted one with good morning and trilled kisses when she said *beijos*. We bought chocolate and cheese – items which had been scarce in Benguela but which we now regularly enjoyed. My mother appeared to be in command of herself, but one day in the midst of proceedings, felt faint and had to sit down. We were in the middle of the fish market and the fishwives abandoned their posts to help her. She resisted, made little of this spell of giddiness. I meanwhile stared at the catches of prawns and fish and the fisherwomen themselves who were spread-eagled on their jute mats and waving flies from their wares. If I looked, and I could not help myself, I could see the dark cavities between their legs and wondered if rivers of blood flowed from them too. Soon my mother recovered, brushed her weakness off, said it must be due to the change in climate from Benguela, and continued how watermelons which came from the Congo were sweeter and more mellow than the watermelons from Angola...Her voice trailing, I soon found myself on the far side of the market amidst the old women selling sausage and salt pork. The area was rank with the stench of smoke and cat piss; litters multiplied each week and the kittens meowed and curled in between the cool stone tablets of the auction blocks. I wanted to take one home with me, but my mother had forbidden me to touch them. Now I stopped to caress one, a runt; it was fractious and leapt from my hands. When I turned back I could no longer see my mother. At first the delirious pleasure of finding myself completely free overcame me. What did it matter where my mother was? I thought I could find her if I wanted but right then had no desire to do so! How exciting to be observing all the things about me without her asides! It was nearly Carnaval and in one corner of the market a ventriloquist had set himself up on a beer crate; the puppet's wasted legs fell over his own and, despite the slightly parted lips which betrayed the simulation, the ventriloquist's string of dirty jokes appeared to issue directly from the puppet's wooden orifice. I looked for a long time before plucking up the courage to approach one of the *bruxas*. She was counting the crumpled banknotes in her rusty tin, surrounded by small bottles whose contents seemed half-evaporated, as well as seeds and dried salt fish and plants laid out to sell as curatives. I looked at her feet, noting that they were for all intents and purposes anatomically correct, when she said, in Kimbundu, something that I could not understand. Then she clapped her hands and spoke again in Portuguese: What do you say, Cleopatra? She was chewing kola and her mouth, stained scarlet with the juices, looked like a gash. Someone admonished the ventriloquist to stop but he had the puppet repeat the threats like a game of echoes. A scuffle broke out and soon a policeman arrived to break up the crowd. Everyone was speaking at once and my temples throbbed to hear them. Near to where I was standing a woman was plaiting *zimbo* shells into bags much like the one that my mother carried. I made my way from one aisle to another where the mountains of dried cassava and maize cast tall shadows across my path. Each time I came to the end of a row of stalls, it was as though I was in a bad dream in which the wares displayed had been switched to disorient me. I slipped and someone laughed at my falling. At one moment I thought I saw my mother in the butchery area. The heads of lambs had been hung up for fast sale; flies swarmed about the lakes of their eyes and threads of blood stained the flagstones. I had mistaken her for a *mestiça* with straightened hair. I knew we were to go to the tailor to pick up a dress that had been stitched for my birthday so I made my way there by myself, crossing the street to his little shop on Rua de Sousa Coutinho, out the front of which there was a concrete bench on which I sat and watched the people going by. Soon I saw my mother coming toward me, shouting my name. When she found me, she said that I could have died crossing the street without her. Tears welled in her eyes and smudged her *kohl*... The tailor was a small, tubercular man, bent over a Singer machine. He had dubbed my mother Marie Antoinette and me her lady-in-waiting. He got up to greet us as soon as he saw her; and when he brought out the dress with white heart-shaped buttons down the front, I was captivated by the fabric which we had chosen at Saratoga. It was printed with a picture of a girl and boy accompanied by their mother on a picnic: in the first scene, the girl was portrayed carrying her doll by one arm to a place where her brother was playing with a dog; in the next, the mother was feeding the children iced cakes and tea; in the final tableau, the father was holding the car door open for the little boy to climb in, to go home. The girl on the fabric was wearing a dress made of the self-same fabric and this story-inside-the-story intrigued me no end. I was so enthralled by the easy domestic enjoyment of this family that I barely caught on when, while my mother paid him, the tailor said that not every child who does not talk is demented but some turn out to be. From the corner of my eye I looked at the tailor: I now decided that he had a smile that I did not like. When he smiled I could see how few teeth he had left in his mouth and that they were all rotten. Then I looked at my mother: she too was smiling and still very beautiful. She put the change in her purse, thanked the tailor and took my hand. We had not gone far though when she suddenly broke step with me. She said that the tailor was right and that people took me for a deaf-mute. She said that the problem was that she had cosseted me far too long. All these things she said with a look of such disappointment that she seemed an utter stranger…That I was not the cause of her disappointment was suddenly apparent to me, but when I turned my head back to see where it may have begun, it was indistinct, there was no clear picture of it. And when I strained ahead to see where it might also end, I could see far out across the sea and to the petrels gliding on the crests of the waves and I could even see the horizon, but I could not see where her unhappiness might end…On the Avenida de Álvaro Ferreira she asked Caetano to stop at a café where we could have cool drinks. We were being seated, when we suddenly saw Papá at another table across the floor, deep in conversation with Senhor Mascarenhas. My father was supposed to be out of town and seemed startled when he caught sight of us. He approached our table, greeting us with a formality by which even Senhor Mascarenhas seemed embarrassed. Senhor Mascarenhas insisted on paying for our drinks and then he and Papá accompanied us to the car. I looked behind me, I looked in front of me and then looked sidelong at my mother. Her head was held high but she had begun to weep; the *kohl* ran down with her tears, staining her face. And although I thought she was still beautiful, it was as a stranger seen in passing, a person who makes quite an impression in the moment but whom you have forgotten only seconds after they have gone.

5

I TOOK THIS UNHAPPY LOOK, which my mother continued to bear, to bode ill. Soon enough when I saw her unhappy it would make me feel bewildered and the distance between the beginning of my bewilderment and the beginning of her unhappiness became more immeasurable as I turned my head forward and back, trying to gauge its proportions. Her sadness took many forms: disgruntlement, worry and restlessness among others. She looked this way when one morning she began giving a series of instructions to Ifigênia: Could she see that Papá's shirts were brought in by early afternoon as it looked like there would be a downpour? Could she please remember to wash the floors today? Crio had been upsetting her seedlings and dragging mud inside...In answer to each question, Ifigênia said yes but as I observed this word – yes – passing her lips, it sounded less than decisive. I was eating *funje* sweetened with molasses, one of my favourite things to eat, and Ifigênia was fixing my braids for school. The next day she would be going to visit her family in Cassongue. My mother had given her a suitcase; it had an old TAP sticker peeling off the canvas. I asked Ifigênia how long the train would take to get to Cassongue and she answered, So long that it would do her better not to think about it. She said that the more she thought about it, the longer it would seem…The radio crackled, the clock ticked and the new refrigerator hummed. There were many new things we had acquired on Papá's higher salary since coming to Luanda: a new television, a new settee, a new car…Yet these accoutrements of his success in the Administration unsettled my mother and she often said she missed Benguela and the simple life we had had there. Now she said she was worried about the railways and what the FNLA, finding Ifigênia with her Portuguese and fair complexion, might do. Ifigênia said not to worry, that the FNLA were far from Cassongue and her Portuguese was full of errors, anyway…That galled my mother and she said that I ought to find another companion than Ifigênia as she was a busy lady. Ifigênia finished tying my braids and went into the yard to collect the washed clothes. My mother was wearing a pair of old *kolhapuris* and the polish had begun to peel off her toenails. She absentmindedly brushed her earlobe and realised she had lost an earring. She began to rummage on the table in a quest for it. She looked under the newspaper, then retraced her steps down the hallway. She called out that the house was in such a state that it was impossible to find anything. She came into the kitchen again and put her hand to her hair and released a sharp cry, flicking something which she must have thought was an insect but in fact was the mislaid earring: it shuttled across the linoleum and she picked it up and put it on. Unblinkingly, she now told me to hurry because we would be late for our appointment at the doctor's in Luanda. She had not said anything about going to the doctor's before; she had merely said we were going to meet with a nun at the Sisters of St Joseph school to which I would be going after Christmas, a time that was far enough away that it seemed like an eternity to me. That my mother might conceal things was something I was beginning to learn. For so many years, I had been like a little bird, gobbling the food, words and ideas, that she put directly into my mouth, already half-masticated. Now I began to consider what was real and what was not, what pleased me and what did not; I began dividing the world this way before swallowing...My mother glanced at the clock and said to eat up; she said that we hadn't all day. In my haste, I spilled the *funje*. She clicked her teeth and said that I needed to learn to be more careful and that sloppiness did not become me. Her impatience gave her face a disfiguring quality, one from which I wanted to turn my eyes – out of shame but also because there was something unsightly in it. In the same tone, she now asked Ifigênia, who had just come in with a basket of clothes, what she was standing about idling for, could she not see that the floor needed to be washed?...The head nun at the Sisters of St Joseph school showed us to the classroom which would soon be my own. She was kind, her face craggy with age. She ushered me to a nativity scene which had been made by the other children in one corner of the room; mute little clay statues of Jesus and Mary, the shepherd and three kings, as well the angels, crowded into the makeshift stable...She said if I sang her a carol, I could place the small figurine of the baby Jesus in the manger, though he would only be born at Christmas. I sang the first lines of 'O Menino está dormindo' and she seemed well pleased. My mother was looking out the window, distracted...Later, in the waiting room of the doctor's surgery, there was a chilled water bottle with a dispenser of paper cups and, after pulling one out, I made the discovery that the cups were automatically replenished. I carried on performing this miracle with the cups until my mother looked daggers at me. When we were called in to see him the doctor gave me two shots – one for diphtheria and one for sleeping sickness. He told my mother that there was nothing at all wrong with me, that I would start talking soon enough – that they should only be sure that they spoke Portuguese not Konkani to me at home. Then the doctor asked my mother to lie down and began examining her; he spoke in a low voice and my mother moaned. I looked out through the window and I suddenly saw the *mestiça* nurse who had been sitting at reception coming out of the surgery and, after hopping onto her bicycle, cycling away. My mother was so nervous, she began talking quickly and randomly. She said how pretty the receptionist was and the doctor scratched his bald patch and said that she could do sixty words per minute, which was better than the secretary he had had from the Algarve. There was a Goan doctor, she rambled, was there not, who had found the cure for sleeping sickness? The doctor said yes, he thought it was so...The doctor now spoke to me. He had a wide, friendly face; he was balding and his shiny head reminded me of that of the clown who mimed and sold helium balloons outside the Miramar Cinema. He told me my mother would soon get big; he told me that she was going to have a baby, and I recalled the red balloon which Ifigênia had bought me and which had become full and buoyant when my parents had recently gone to see *Black Orpheus*. To stop myself from crying, I now concentrated on the eye chart with its fractured alphabet written in smaller and smaller letters. If I squinted I could make out even the bottommost line. There was a poster for Benadryl in which a child gleefully gulped the red elixir that his voluptuous mother, so blonde as to have been

Scandinavian, spoon-fed him…Now when I looked at her again my mother had been transformed into the attractive stranger. She smiled at the doctor and, taking my hand, smiled at me. I hardly imagined that I would be able to meet her in her treachery but by contorting my lips and straining all the muscles of my face I returned the compliment, I produced my own smile. Did it distress me to smile so falsely at her? Perhaps I was a good impersonator, her very own protégée. On our way out the doctor gave me a bull's eye; the lolly was stale and melted at once in my mouth. My mother began walking ahead of me and there was not a great distance between us to begin with, but for every one step she took I had to take two, otherwise I would be trailing her. Having made the calculation, I refused to take that second step so that the distance in time got greater and, when she called to me that I should not lag behind, I pretended I could not hear her. She had Ifigênia set up the bed in the front room and told me that I would now be sleeping there alone. She said it was high time, and besides, I would soon be a big sister. As night fell, she led me to my new bedroom and our shadows redoubled on the walls. I sat on the edge of the bed, palms upturned on my lap, watching the silhouettes duplicate; when they met, they made the outline of a lurid chimera. If the baby was a girl she would be called Madalena; if a boy, she told me that he would be called Henrique after Papá. She turned back the sheets and leant in to kiss me and her face, full as the moon may have been full, was so close that it eclipsed everything. When she left, I lay awake for some time. The bed was narrow and I turned from one side to another, unable to lie naturally in any one place. The temperature dropped and I grew cold. When I fell asleep, my dreams were strange and turbulent. I woke in the night to find my mother was not there and in the morning glimpsed my reflection in the long armoire mirror. The mirror was framed by blue and white *azulejo* tiles painted with tiny windmills. I saw my two eyes, dark and elongated; the shiny crown of my hair; my nose, long and with a wide bridge like Papá's; my dark and bushy brow, and the gold sleepers that had been threaded through my earlobes in the weeks after I was born. My face, belonging to another landscape, one I did not know, gave me the thrill of unexpected discovery and for some moments I moved my mouth, I sang to myself, not in any language that had been taught me, not a lullaby for a messiah but a song of my own improvisation, maybe discordant, but a song more comforting than real words might have offered.

6

WHEN THE BABY WAS BORN DEAD, I was at school. That morning I had been told by the teacher, an ex-nun from Coimbra, to stand with my hands on my head at the front of the classroom, for what misdemeanour I was not entirely sure, although I had begun to find myself in this posture more and more frequently. The teacher from Coimbra had earlier asked which of us had heard of Bartolomeu Dias. No one answered, but it so happened that I had recently heard a broadcast on Emissora Católica about Che Guevara meeting Agostinho Neto. It was reported that they recited poetry together and Guevara had told Neto that Dias was an invader…I was sitting at the kitchen table, eating the lion's share of the fried plantains Ifigênia had put before me, when I heard the broadcaster's indignant declaration: Invader! When the teacher from Coimbra asked who had heard of Bartolomeu Dias, I had therefore repeated, loudly, that he was the invader. At first surprised that I had spoken at all, she grew displeased. Her face became a confusion of piety and furious patriotism and all the edifices of knowledge and faith that until then been holding her up seemed to give way beneath her. She hovered over my desk before pulling me up by the arm to the front of the class. She proceeded to make an example of me, pointing first to the map of the world, then to the portrait of Salazar above the chalkboard and finally to the crucifix on the wall above the door. The other girls were mirthful and whispering and she clapped her hands to silence them. Her voice tremulous, she declared that Bartolomeu Dias had been commissioned by João II and Isabel; she said that he had battled storm and shipwreck and cannibalism to claim Angola for Portugal. Bartolomeu Dias, she said, was responsible for civilising the people of Angola and was part of that long line of *fidalgos* who had cultivated my own loinclothed and mud-thatched and blue-godded people! When she had made this speech, the teacher from Coimbra was standing close to me and yet it seemed I could not see her; her face was a blur. When she spoke, her breath smelt stale – as of onions and salt pork sitting in a pot too long. Not a day went by without one girl or other being humiliated by her, so I tried not to take this humiliation to heart. There was a rumour that the husband of the teacher from Coimbra – for whom she had left the convent and run away to Angola – had in turn left her and gone to the interior of the country to live with a native woman who was a Jehovah's Witness. I now struggled to make out the defining characteristics of the teacher from Coimbra: her clothes were out of style and inappropriate for the Luandan climate – long woollen skirts, blouses that buttoned high at her neck and thick stockings. A patina of make-up turned between morning and midday to a crust on her pale, perspiring face. Her hands were never still but always nervously wringing and her nails bitten to the quick. Looking closely at her I thought, it is heartbreak that has defined her, and resolved at once that I would never allow such a thing to happen to me. What do you have to say for yourself? the teacher from Coimbra now rounded on me and demanded when she came to the end of her homage to Bartolomeu Dias. Up until now it was true I had little to say. Who was I? How had I come here? Such simple facts of geography and history went right over my head...My arms itched from the bites I had got sitting in my room the previous night, picking out fleas from Crio's belly and crushing them between my fingers, and now I scratched them furiously. I had hiccups, for I had eaten my lunch quickly, and now that the teacher from Coimbra had finished releasing hers, I could not stop myself from breaking my own, sweet wind. I did not feel anger about the punishment meted out on me and neither did I feel remorse. In the surface of the streaky glass of the portrait of Salazar before which I stood with my hands on my head, paying the penalty for farting before the teacher from Coimbra, I could see her reflection; I could see the reflection of the girls who stood in their checked uniforms and long socks, mechanically chorusing the national anthem with the teacher from Coimbra's voice tunelessly leading, 'Heroes of the sea, noble people, valiant nation and immortal, lift today again Portugal's splendour...' I could hear the crows outside, cawing, cawing. A worker carried a bucket of lime across the compound to whitewash the statue of São José. Once or twice, the lime splashed out of the bucket. The wind coming off the sea swept dust about and sunlight now and again glinted through the palm fronds. Time passed but I was not aware how much time... Losing circulation at the front of the classroom, I began to have a vision. It was not a vision worthy of beatification but it stopped me as I imagine the three children ambling, their stomachs grumbling with hunger, were stopped in the valley of Cova da Iria in the days before the outbreak of World War I.

The vision involved the mistress of the husband of the teacher from Coimbra. I imagined her sitting on the porch of a house in a quiet valley near the Cuanza River. It was bruxa to cut your nails after dark, as the clippings would fly into the air unseen and blind your enemy, and that is what the mistress of the husband of the teacher from Coimbra was doing as she sat on the porch with the mist rising. When the vision had come and gone, it was not the Blessed Virgin or the teacher from Coimbra but the kindly head nun standing behind me. Her secret did not overwhelm me; her revelation did not culminate in a transfiguration. The head nun led me out of the classroom and, putting her hands on my small shoulders, simply told me that the baby had been born dead. The baby was born dead, she repeated…I recalled seeing a girl coming out of the swimming pool on Rua de Salvador Correia; when she had removed her swimming cap, her long blonde hair had fallen down her back and I wondered whether the same happened when the head nun pulled the wimple from her head at night to bathe. Papá was waiting at the school gates; he had tears in his eyes. Yet when he embraced me it was as though he were not embracing a human being at all, but something spectral. Henrique died, he said, and I imagined a tiny form with bright brown eyes that opened and closed like a doll…My ears popped in the elevator that took us up many floors in the Maternidade Maria do Carmo Vieira Machado. The walls were white and vast, in the old colonial style. Nurses shuffled past in their rubber-soled shoes, whispering earnestly. Many women were asleep; some sat up knitting or talking to other patients; a few nursed babies. When the nurse accompanying us stopped at the entrance to a ward and pointed my mother out, she was lying against the pillows looking out the window, a copy of *Time* magazine on her lap. When I called to her, she turned to me slowly, as in a film when two people who have been parted are unexpectedly reunited with each other, but the nearer I came the more it seemed she was staring beyond me, as though it were not me she were waiting for but someone else, someone who may never have arrived but for whom she would always be lifting her eyes, feeling her heart quickening. Free of its weight, her belly rose and fell. She told me that little Henrique would be put in a coffin and laid in the earth at the cemetery. The Alto das Cruzes cemetery was on the plateau of Rua de São Tomé. Planes from the airport took off nearby and hovered above it. I imagined standing at the cemetery surrounded by a concatenation of airplanes. Ifigênia would wear her good dress of blue serge, and Caetano one of Papá's old suits. Papá would perhaps cry again and the tear drops would fall and shine the tips of his brogues. Senhor Mascarenhas would be standing away in the distance...I wondered whether little Henrique would really be in the coffin, or whether it would be empty? I might be tempted to knock on it, to open the lid to see if Henrique, like Lazarus, might come out of the tomb, clean-shaven and lithe of limb? Would little Henrique come to meet me in my dreams; would he come to summon me to the world of the dead?...In the days and weeks afterward, I found that all I had to do was think of him and he suddenly appeared. Yet he was not filled out: he was notional, with a notional head of hair and notional eyes, a notional body and a notional sex, all of which could appear and disappear as mercurially as an idea. When I went outside to take my nightie off the line, little Henrique got into a tug of war in which the nightie was the casualty. When I brushed my teeth and wiggled a tooth that had been aching, Henrique naturally appeared to mock me in the mirror. When no one was looking it was little Henrique who swiped money from the bowl on the sideboard. Only when I called his name in my dreams did Henrique keep his distance. Though I invoked his name, he lurked further and further away from me. I chased him, the soles of my bare feet becoming broken on the surface of the rocks they traversed. I got up, only to fall down again and my mother appeared. What are you doing up? she asked and put me back to bed. Her hair was cropped short like a boy's and her breasts were full of milk. Experiencing discomfort in the middle of the night she wandered restlessly through the house. Because she slept so far into the morning, Ifigênia prepared me for school, braiding and making coils of the braids on either side of my head. When I came home my mother was still in her nightgown, which was loose about her shoulders, and her feet were bare and dirty. She drank tea out of many cups and the empty cups were scattered about the house, a portrait of her mental state. She locked the pantry and took to keeping the key behind the icebox, muttering darkly about thieves. She ate almost nothing and would complain about Ifigênia's cooking. When she passed my bedroom, she flew into a rage if my bed was badly made or the pillow out of place. She stopped reading books and took to carrying the Bible around, arbitrarily spouting passages from Proverbs. One evening I sat sucking a kola nut and completing my sums on the kitchen table. Though I had concealed it in my cheek, she asked me where I had got the kola nut. I answered that a school friend, Susana, had plucked it from a bush on the way back from school and given it to me. I launched into an

elaborate description of the fictional bush, burning with a sur-
plus of kola nuts, at the end of which she opened the palm of
her hand and I spat it out; a thread of red saliva unravelled
with it. Incidentally, she said, kola doesn't grow here, it grows
in Ambriz, so either you are lying or you have a fertile imagination. She said that I had grown sly; she said that I had turned
into a person she no longer trusted. She pulled the bands from
the end of my braids and began snaking her fingers through to
loosen them. The following morning when she saw me saying
goodbye to Ifigênia at the school gates, Susana asked me why
my servant was the one to drop me off, and I told her my little
brother had died, whereupon she slipped her hand sympathet-
ically into mine. It was a great consolation and by the end of
the day I had persuaded her to give me a rare marine stamp
from São Tomé.

7

ON ALL SAINTS DAY we went on excursion to the Ilha de Luanda. The sand of the Ilha was white and fine, like the beach at Porto Amboim where we had holidayed when I was small. There were people picnicking but we could not go into the water because oil had spilled from an Egyptian tanker that morning creating a slick for kilometres. Susana's little sister, Inês, did not understand the danger and kept running toward the sea. Her mother lumbered after her and tried to reason with her – but this was little use, for when we had our heads turned, she would head off again toward the water...There were so many soldiers stationed on the fort; from afar they looked like toy soldiers. One of them caught up with her and carried Inês back to where we were. When the soldier had gone, her mother struck Inês across the face. Susana looked away ashamed and so did some others nearby, yet no one protested against this act of cruelty and little Inês herself seemed well acquainted with it; she only folded up her legs, rocked and murmured quietly to herself. I turned over the insight – that those who hurt you may be the same who otherwise claimed to protect your interests and care for you – and did not fail to speak my thoughts about it to Susana at the next opportunity. We were in the perfect conspiratorial setting, collecting *zimbo* shells; Susana looked out over the water and said her mother was upset because their servant girl, Milagre, had run away. Then she said, We may have to go home to South Africa because of the war. Which war? I asked her. I don't know, she shrugged. Her parents often argued about it and her father had lately threatened to sell his assets, various farms, and a thriving cotton export business; there was her uncle in Cape Town who would help them…She squinted into the sun and turned away. We walked to the jetty and sat there eating our lunch, a picnic of some *frango* with *piripiri* and bread. The other girls were turning cartwheels and writing their names in the wet sand, watching the waves crash over and erase what they had written. They would provoke the head nun by throwing handfuls of sand at each other and then feigning innocence. In the afternoon, the fishermen took us out on the water. I looked at the boards beneath my sandals; they were very worn so I could see through to the earlier layers of green and grey paint which had peeled away – and between the boards the swirling dark waters of the Atlantic…As we rounded the tip of the Cabo, I turned back to look at the façade of the São Miguel fort. There were wild rumours about it – that it was haunted, that the ghost of the poet Camões was there and that it was his cyclopean blinker that was seen encircling the sea from the fort's high tower – but in fact there was nothing spectacular about it; it seemed to be just a tower distributing light across water. I wondered whether de Novais and the sailors of the Discoveries sometimes saw humpbacks, and how, taken from their native towns in the Alentejo, they might have trembled to be out on the sea alone with them; how at night, with the sea dark and vast and only the light of the southern stars to orient them, the sky itself different to the sky of home, they must have prayed that their own seasickness might end. I gazed at the statue of the Blessed Virgin who had from her vantage point on the Carmo looked on as so many slaves had been pressed into ships that would take them to Brazil, so that the ancient tribes of Angola were lost on another continent, to say nothing of the dispossession of the Indians and the forests of Brazil cleared for the sugar plantations that the slaves were forced to work. I wondered what home may mean and what different routes one might take to get there. I was watching the water churning, wondering what secrets that sea could disclose, how much fear and loss, and how much expectation. I was wondering whether life itself was a terrible unmooring, when I felt the bile suddenly curdle in my stomach and I retched over the boat railing…At low tide we could see the local fishermen coming back, their small boats brimming with dorado, but the rainbow-coloured fish they'd caught were now contaminated with the dark oil and the fisherman were busy discarding them. I clasped the *zimbo* shells we had collected like a talisman. A man was selling *pé de moleque* and Susana's mother gave us money for some. When we returned from Ilha de Luanda it was dusk. My mother was in the garden. She loved to be here, with Crio curled up beside her, working quietly into the evening. Everything was in flower: the white flowers of the moringa, the fuchsia petals of the bougainvillea, the star jasmine and the frangipani whose scent entered and permeated the whole house. She wore a kaftan and an old yellow sun hat from Benguela times; its wide brim drooped over her face. For old times' sake, I covered her eyes and bent to kiss her and she exclaimed, My little wanderer has returned! But it suddenly felt insincere, a game, something we said before company…Ifigênia passed by on her way out to collect the washing and Susana's mother started pacing. She said she could not think why their servant girl, Milagre, had up and left; she had searched all of Luanda and even sent a telegram to her parents in Moçâmedes. Who knows, she said, perhaps Milagre had fallen pregnant to one of the workers on the construction site behind their house? Inês was playing with Crio and my mother told me to take Susana to my room. In my bedroom, I asked if she'd like to play a game, buraco or canasta, or we could play Discoveries. This last was one of our own games, and not much could be said of its rules, except that it involved my leaving Susana with one of her possessions. I was so adept at it that I had in the last months appropriated a Swiss chalet paperweight in which snow appeared to fall when it was upturned or shaken; a silver bracelet now missing one of its glossy moonstones; as well as innumerable stamps from her collection. My favourite treasure was a viewfinder: the large cards slotted in and gave three-dimensional vistas of the Seven Wonders of the World. When I had acquired the viewfinder we had been in Susana's room, a place in which I had come to feel the full glory of my dominion over her, and now here I was, lying on my own bed, clicking forward to the picture of the Pyramids of Giza and back to that of Machu Picchu. Clicking forward and backward, I told Susana how much I loved it, but in reality this game of conquests and all that I had acquired humiliated me. She gave me almost anything I asked, ran to my defence when I was in the wrong, copied my errors and the worst of my behaviour. I would sometimes catch her with her eyes closed, whispering to herself, and when I asked her what she was doing she would tell me with an utter lack of guile that she was praying. In earnest, she now began twisting the gold cross at her neck and describing her Crisma dress. We were standing near the old armoire with the *azulejo* tiles whose tiny blue windmills seemed both beautiful and obscure…From the kitchen, I could hear Emissora Católica and the strains of Sergio Godinho's popular song, 'Falling in Love': 'I sent her a letter on perfumed paper and in beautiful handwriting, I said she had so bright, warm and merry a smile like the November sun…' The singer sent many letters to his sweetheart in which he made ardent declarations of his feelings – all of which were pathetically rebuffed. 'I paid for her sweets at the Mission causeway', Susana began humming the song. I had a brainwave and announced that we too could be lovers. Susana countered that lovers take their clothes off and lie naked with each other. I was talking to her reflection in the mirror and my reflection in turn talked to hers. Okay, I said, and before I knew what was happening, we began removing our clothes. Now what were we to do? I asked. Make babies, she instructed. She said that I would lie on top of her and she would then lie on top of me. She said this was what her father had done to their maid, Milagre. I at first felt an aversion to Susana but then this aversion turned into an aversion to myself and to the whole world and I pulled quickly away. I pursed my lips in distaste. I scolded that either Susana was a liar or she had a fertile imagination. I told her that she had turned into a person I no longer trusted. We got dressed and she looked on bewildered as I began to gather up the paperweight, the bracelet and the viewfinder to give back to her. Just then, we heard footsteps and voices and Susana's long-suffering mother calling her name. At the door, Susana and I brushed cheeks as though nothing had changed between us...As we went inside again my mother asked what game we had been playing. I answered, Making babies. She said that it was a silly game. She said that Susana was silly and her mother was naïve. She said, You want to know how to make a baby? It's too simple! Then she took up the comb from the bureau; the salt and the wind of the Ilha had tangled my hair and she drew the comb through it. The *zimbo* shells were scattered across my bed and, each time she pulled the comb through my hair, I glanced at them. Each time I pulled away from her, I imagined my hair slowly becoming wet with the weight of dark oil. I pulled away from her, for I kept wanting to look at myself, to see if there was dark oil staining my face too. She gave up and ran my bath. Papá arrived home. Ifigênia had prepared *calulu de peixe* and we ate without speaking. There was news of the farm strikes on the radio and he got up in fury to turn it off. He shouted that it was too much to be surrounded by fools. Why did I come to this country of fools? he smashed his fist on the table, rattling the plates, cutlery and glasses. He said that we would not be intimidated, especially not by some so-called Marxists who could not read *Das Kapital*! Night was falling and Crio barked at the nightjars while my mother ate her dinner and then went to her bedroom. When I passed her later, I saw her sitting on the edge of her bed, peeling an apple. She had made one long ribbon of the peel and was humming an old Konkani *mando*:

> Leaving all your friends this way,
> To earn your daily bread you go away...

8

On the morning of my Crisma my mother braided my hair with moringa from the garden. She stood back after plaiting the buds into my hair and, congratulating herself on the work of art which I, lace dress, lace veil, and wearer of her well-tended blossoms had become, said see what a pretty girl I could be. The more often she said such things, the more I resented my sex and the awkward complications of my body. I looked with envy at boys my age, kicking footballs, able to go out late and return whenever they pleased, and swearing in the street. If I were a boy, I believed, I might escape all that those blossoms and my mother's words seemed to prefigure...In her bedroom, my mother opened the lid of her old jewellery box. With its evocative scent of sandal and patchouli, it had once held such a charm, yet now I looked upon the contents with a heavy sense of duty, as a dowry I wished to forsake. She presented me with a gold crucifix; her own mother had given the same to her on the day of her Crisma, she told me, and turned the pendant over to show me the *devanagari* signature of the old goldsmith from Goa, before fastening the chain round my neck...We took polaroids in the garden and Ifigênia gifted me a scapular that had a picture of Santa Teresa of Avila on one side and the Virgin Mary on the other. At the last moment, we found Crio unable to stand properly. In the months before, we had begun to see him bringing up his food. We carried him to his favourite spot – some old, fragrant coffee sacks in the kitchen – and he keened plaintively. Papá said he would soon have to be put down and my mother and I both cried. Then she reapplied her *kohl* and composed herself, creating a face to present to the world. On the way to the cathedral, the hair pins with which the stems of the moringa had been affixed to my hair came loose. When I put my hand to my head to secure them, the blossoms fell out. The Crisma dress was too tight; I had grown a lot since the time I had been measured for it, and my feet hurt in the taut leather of the new shoes, though they were one size larger than I needed when we bought them. My arms and legs, suddenly ungainly and long – and nearly as obstreperous as my senses – seemed to pull me in all directions. I had not eaten anything that morning and, during the prayers that were said and the long reading from the Acts of the Apostles, I grew impatient. The priest read: 'And when the day of the Pentecost was fully come, they were all with one accord in one place… And there appeared unto them cloven tongues like as of fire, and it sat upon each of them. And they were all filled with the Holy Ghost, and began to speak with other tongues, as the Spirit gave them utterance.' I was sweating profusely. When I looked up, I saw the old fan rotating at its ancient pace; threads of cobwebs lifted lightly from the beams and dust motes danced before the amber-coloured lozenges of the stained-glass windows. I looked at Susana who was sitting with her family in the opposite row, praying in earnest. Just a few weeks earlier I had been sitting in much the same position, practising for this moment; then as now I had felt nothing at all; then as now, about to accept the blessing of the Holy Spirit, all I felt was a kind of numbness, a fraudulence. I fixed my gaze on the sixth station of the cross in which Veronica, wearing a red velvet gown, skin cherubic, held up her veil for Christ to wipe his brow. I looked closely at the muslin of the veil which contained a ghostly imprint of Christ's face…Who was the artist, a native presumably, who had painted Veronica in this pose, I wondered and my eye traversed the entire Way of Sorrows: Jesus meeting his mother; Simon of Cyrene helping Jesus carry the cross; Jesus falling the second time; Jesus meeting the women of Jerusalem. How such a story, the terrible spectacle of a man's torture and suffering, could be said to be redemptive, I failed to understand. 'Our Father who art in Heaven', the congregation now faithfully recited, and I wondered how a god, said to also be among us in spirit, and of whose flesh we were apparently to partake too, might really have accepted that the cathedral itself was built in his name with the labour of so many enslaved natives. Or that the *musseques* of the homeless were only a stone's throw from the cathedral. My mother had told me to look away but it was precisely in that direction, to what was unseemly rather than sanctified, that I was drawn. My own name, Maria-Cristina, in fact said everything and nothing about who I was or my origins; I could have been given any other name – Isabel, Elisabete, Fernanda – it now occurred to me…and how different my fate might have been had my ancestors fled into the hills with their gods. There was a children's book by which I was enchanted when I was small and which I had recently uncovered in my bookshelf. It was a book of stories from the *Mahabharata*. My favourite was that of Shakuntala, born among birds, who, when abandoned by her husband, Dashuntya, takes her young son and rears him in a wild part of the forest. I loved the part of the story that told how Shakuntala's son Bharata was so astute with the animals he would coax the wild tigers and lions to open their mouths so he could count their teeth. I would ask my mother to stop and reread this passage to me. I thought, I should like to take that name, Shakuntala, rather than that of Saint Teresa, whose story I had been learning by heart in preparation for my Crisma. For I should feel more kinship with such a woman, born among birds, who escaped to a forest to raise her child alone in the wild, than one who had spent her life cloistered in a cell of a convent, meditating on mortal sin and subjecting herself to deliberate tortures – even if the result was a kind of spiritual ecstasy. These thoughts swirled round and, with each new one, I kept sweating some more. I felt faint as the priest held the host aloft and broke it; as he took it into his mouth and feverishly swallowed it; as he gulped the wine from the chalice. Soon the initiates began to pour into the aisles and I knew I should go ahead. As I did, I began to worry that blood had overflowed and stained my dress. I had been keeping the secret from my mother for some time and now could not do other than whisper what I feared. She frowned, dismayed that I should wait for such an occasion to say so…It was not so bad though, as I saw after the ceremony when we arrived at one of the large mansions on the Praia do Bispo where there was a party. I went to the bathroom. The blood was there, like sticky black tar, but there was not so much of it as I had imagined. Susana was standing away, under a large palm tree. She invited me to Cape Town, where she would soon be going to join her uncle's family. I felt I was making a false promise when I said yes, for

I knew I would probably never see her again and had already begun to distance myself from the pain of this knowledge by pretending not to care. This did not have the desired effect, for she misted up and embraced me. The truth was that I had abandoned Susana for the friendship of another girl, Andrea, whose party it was. Her father was a senior official in the Consulate General of the Union of South Africa and went on one diplomatic mission after another. Her mother spent her days throwing parties and having treatment in a clinic in Amsterdam for the terrible depressions which coincided with her father's absence. Andrea was very beautiful, with dark hair, pale freckled skin and piercing blue eyes. She played piano virtuosically and invariably came first in class, yet needed constant reassurance. Now she asked me to come swim in the pool. I told Andrea I was bleeding. She laughed, Oh, the curse, and said to come in anyway. I followed her into the pool but I became self-conscious and then got out again…She stretched her legs in front of her and told me how she had started to shave them without her mother knowing; later she would show me how. She bit the split ends from her hair and said there were a lot of things she did not tell her mother. She was in love with an older boy, Miguel, a friend of her brother's, who managed a ship-wright's factory and now she pointed Miguel out to me and speculated about her prospects with him. As she kept talking, I looked up and saw the clouds; they moved ever so slowly but if I slowed my mind too I could observe them moving infinitesimally…We got up and went inside and, as we neared the top of the stairs, we met Andrea's mother on her way down. Her halter top hung low, her makeup was smudged and she appeared to trip a little on the stairs. Bangles jangled on her nervous wrists. She was smoking and the ash from her cigarette tumbled lightly to the carpeted floor. I noticed her teeth were stained yellow from tobacco and she had a slight gap between them. As she started to speak she slurred her speech and I realised she was drunk. What a lovely complexion, she said, touching my cheek. Your family are from Goa? she asked, then before I could answer that I had never been there, she went on to say she would like to go one day. Are there coconut groves and do the Hindu women commit ritual suicide on the funeral pyres of their husbands? Is it true there are sacred cows that chew their cud in the middle of the road? I said there were no roads as far as I knew…Anyway, go and have some cake, she cut me off, it's simply delicious. We balanced plates of the Crisma cake on our knees in the front room where the other guests had gathered, eating *quitaba* and watching footage of Benfica scoring a goal. The television did not give a perfect picture but everyone looked on in silence, captivated by the sight of Jaime Graça soaring through the air and making an unexpected comeback for the side. Someone changed the channel; General Kaúlza was being interviewed, talking about battlelines being drawn, and another guest shouted to change it back to the football. The mood changed from merriment and a fight soon broke out, with two drunks lunging at each other and the crowd scattering. It was humid; lights glittered about the pool. Andrea told me to telephone to ask if I could stay overnight, but when I called my mother I asked her to take me home. I said that Andrea was a flirt, only interested in boys and that her mother let her have too much liberty. My mother said there were plenty of such girls in this world. She said girls with self-respect were nowadays hard to come by. I returned and sat next to

Andrea, hung my head and said, My mother is a real monster! Well, Andrea said, linking arms with me, Never mind, maybe next time. We turned back to the television screen and she said, You think your mother's a monster? and then started to catalogue her own mother's flaws and vices. I was not quite listening; my mind had begun wandering again, for out of the corner of my eye I had noticed the man after Andrea's heart, Miguel, sitting on a cushion on the opposite side of the room. He kept sipping from his bottle of Cuca and licking the chilli of the *quitaba* from his lips. Now when he stood up to get a beer he smiled and I looked away, indignant, before breaking into a smile too. I was still smiling when my mother came with Caetano to collect me, but this smile disappeared as we entered the house because I realised Crio was gone. While we were gone, my father had taken him outside, shot him and buried him in the garden.

9

WE WERE SPARING WITH OIL, with sugar, with gas, and yet there was always a scarcity. Every day there was news of plantation closures and all over the neighbourhood signs of apartments being vacated. My mother would take Alka-Seltzers and go to bed early. Of a morning, she would glance at the pages of *Journal de Angola* then look quickly away…She quarrelled with Ifigênia about expenses, after which Ifigênia went to her people; when overnight the railway route from Lobito became a target we had no idea when she would return. My mother retreated into the past then, perhaps she had nowhere else to go, opening photo albums and taking out old letters: reminiscing. She showed me photographs of the old house in Goa, the church, the paddy fields, the hills surrounding the village and the wide river that ran through it. She taught me a *dekhni* about the river and crossing it and the refrain that went, 'These anklets from my feet, do take them, do take them…' She told me of the Carmelite convent she had schooled at when she was a girl and the nuns who had taught her – Latin, maths, how to stitch. Portuguese stitches, she said, drawing an inscrutable figure in the air. At one time she had wanted to be a nun, she now laughed. And yet, she said she did not know which was a better fate – to devote oneself to God or to a husband. The nuns were clever, capable of such practical and worldly things, yet no doubt they had their sorrows – poverty and terrible family secrets…Her father was from a well-known Brahmin family, a lawyer like Papá, but he had died of tuberculosis when my mother was just eight years old. After that, land disputes with her father's brothers had erupted. Often enough these uncles would bring gifts of food or labourers, only to remind my mother and grandmother that the house they lived in was not theirs. Sometimes they were so desperate my mother would have to walk to her uncles' houses to get the takings from the paddy – a humiliation which she would try to lessen by wearing her best clothes. As a teenager, she had fallen in love with a Hindu boy, Sanjay, the brother of her best friend, Meeta. They made a pact to be together whatever happened, but her mother soon discovered the relationship and determined to separate them. Still, they were hopeful: things were rapidly changing and there was talk of the Portuguese leaving. She and Sanjay schemed to run away to Bombay together, but on the eve of their departure, he joined the liberation army and eventually only his letters to her came from the border with Maharashtra…It was then that my grandmother made the approach to my father's family, wealthy Brahmins from a neighbouring village. Papá promised to take my mother away to Angola, and to make a fortune there. The Portuguese were leaving Goa, anyway, he said…Nehru would plunder all the foreign reserves. His words carried my mother away from her own mother, from the man she really loved, from everything known and familiar. How could she have known that more than any foreign country or continent, her husband would be the region she would be least capable of understanding? When the time came, she had no choice but to take the vow by which she was handed from one family to another...Perhaps she had never left Goa, she said, turning the pages of her wedding album, in which she looked so beautiful and so sad. For many months after they had arrived and set up house in Benguela, my mother tried to forget everything. She was glad for the oceans that existed between her present and her past, she said, so vast, deep and unfathomable, nothing could wash ashore. But then she got the news of Sanjay being killed in the war in Kashmir...Now she warned me not to be vain: she said, beauty ends, and looking at her I could see how this may be true; how her face, once beautiful, with the addition of suffering had become like a mirror of that suffering. However far away you go, she said, you will always be my daughter...It was meant to be a seed sown in the garden of some maternal idyll to say that nothing could come between us. Yet secretly, I dared to think that I, with my legs that had become long and shapely, my hips that had swelled, my breasts that had grown full and firm, had taken her place in the sun. Each month, though I would prefer to forget it, blood flowed out of me with unfailing regularity, reminding me of what I would one day choose: to bear a child or not bear a child. I sweated and, from under my arms, the smell was at once vinegary and sweet. When I lay down, I felt my body stirring with the most intimate longings and associations. I had bought some earrings, little painted wooden birds, at the night bazaar on Rua do Visconde; despite the irritation they caused, I could not bear to remove them. Now as I scratched at my earlobes, my mother said I should change them back to the gold sleepers she had given me. I had applied lipstick to my lips and *kohl* to my eyes; she said I had smudged it and she would show me how to reapply it. I was wearing a midriff top Andrea had given me with jeans, and my mother said I would be inviting unwanted attention. I wanted to say that attention was exactly what I wanted to invite. I wanted to say that should I too have a womb whose soil was rich and fertile – if a girl should one day grow there, with small breasts like buds, with a sex soft and moist as a lily – I would feed her plentifully of the Tree of Life, since it seemed just as tempting and delicious as that of the Knowledge of Good and Evil. Instead I brushed past her and headed to the door. As I left, I could hear her calling out to bring back some green chillies and a few limes – she wanted to make *cafreal*. I crossed the garden, passing Caetano who was listening to the MPLA news broadcast from Brazzaville. I walked along the familiar streets of our neighbourhood and then further until I had reached the city. I stopped at the foot of the statue of Vasco da Gama in Largo de Pedro Alexandrino, listening to the old accordion player from Príncipe playing that *fado*, 'The Boat', which was a favourite in his repertoire. Soldiers surrounded Largo do Infante Dom Fernando; some had been sent from Lisbon to make up local cohorts. They were unused to the heat and so the Miramar Cinema was crowded with off-duty soldiers from the square. I watched people entering and leaving the cinema: couples mostly, smiling and buying cones of *quitaba* and ice-creams. I was standing in the queue to buy an ice-cream when an *alferes*, a *mestiço*, offered to buy me a ticket. I followed him into the cinema and I sat next to him when he tried to kiss me and put my hand on his crotch. I was shocked but throughout the film, *Fiddler on the Roof*, on which I could hardly concentrate, I found that I could not say whether I wanted to remove my hand or keep it there

and, while weighing up both possibilities, I felt his sex grow big.
I did not know what to do: keep my hand on his sex, or take it
away. In this way I grew to make him look desperate, beside
himself. His beret sat on his lap, concealing everything and
nothing. When we came out of the cinema we parted almost
immediately; the shame I felt was as strange as it was new but
not altogether repugnant…I craned my neck and watched
him, lighting a Definitivo and walking briskly through the
archway of the cinema. In the light of day – his face pock-
marked, his hair shorn in the fashion of the Portuguese Legion,
his epaulets shining – he seemed so aloof and arrogant, whereas in the darkness and close to me he had seemed so vulnerable. Now I looked about for him but he had soon merged with
the crowds. I went to the small black-and-white photograph
booth and took a strip of portraits of myself. The photographs
took some minutes to be processed and when I looked, I could
hardly recognise myself, the smudged *kohl* and the little wooden
birds looked so garish. I was crossing into the square when
shots suddenly rang out – people screamed and fled then after
some moments cautiously gathered round. Two soldiers tried
to staunch the wound while another shouted for an ambulance…It was the body of another soldier – not mine, but he
might have been, another *alferes*. Someone said he'd gone mad
– that was why he'd shot himself. I could not stop staring at the
blood that had pooled about his black hair…Some time passed
and I remained there watching as the body was taken away on
a military stretcher. Suddenly someone tapped me on the
shoulder: it was Andrea, with her brother Paulo and the myste-
rious Miguel. We drew back and in silence walked along the
Marginal. The sea was a black abyss and the sky hooded in

cloud. There were few ships in the harbour and we could hear
someone playing the Rui Mingas song that had been banned,
'Monagambé': 'Who wakes up early? Who goes to the ton-
ga?...It is the sweat of my face that waters the plantations.' We
walked to Bairro do Café and the others started talking about
what they had seen. I was nervous, shaking, and couldn't really
speak. Andrea put her arm around me and ordered a coffee.
She said she would teach me to meditate. She pulled her legs
up and said, This is how *sadhus* do it, her mother had shown
her; sometimes they levitated. Her brother rolled his eyes. Sepia photographs – of Pepetela, António Jacinto, Mário Pinto
de Andrade, Viriato da Cruz – covered the wall behind the bar,
great poets and writers, I thought, but for all their eloquence
would they close the growing distance between words and
things? Andrea started arguing with Paulo and Miguel started
speaking to me but it was so loud with all the voices rising in the
café. I made out, What do you think of Pessoa? I said I liked
some of what I had read, which was not very much at all...He
said sometimes he felt like one of Pessoa's alter egos, a wanderer. I said there were a lot of alter egos, so that we hardly
know Pessoa himself, other than as an irresponsible dreamer
who escaped having to be anybody. Miguel then began to re-
cite a poem: 'Once more I see you, City of my horrifyingly lost
childhood...Happy and sad city, once more I dream here...I?
Is it one and the same I who lived here, and came back, And
came back again, and again, And yet again have come back?'
I had heard it before and it was not the words of the poem so
much as the sound of his voice which I suppose stirred
me...I removed the earrings and lay them on the table next to
me and Miguel picked them up, studied them closely and then

smiled at me, complicit. The light faded outside, lights came on in the shop windows opposite and I said I had to be getting home. Miguel said he would drop me on his scooter and I looked to Andrea; she acted insouciant, as though it hardly mattered to her, and laughed in a false manner that reminded me of her mother. As we rode away from the old part of the city, I could see everything very closely, but also, as if from far away, the smaller and larger order of things. Back home, the *cafreal* was ready. I was going to tell my mother about the dead soldier but she had gone to lie down. I went into the bathroom and washed my face; the *kohl* rubbed away with warm water. Caetano came in; there was news that the South African military had been routed in Moxico and we listened to the full story before I brought out plates and served us. The lime of the *cafreal* was tart and the green chilli intensely hot and the flesh of the chicken fell away from the bone. While we ate I thought, here we are, across the table, orphans of Empire...yet in reality Caetano was doubly orphaned, with family on the other side of the continent, in Mozambique, which had already become independent. I remembered how in Benguela he would get apprehensive as he wrapped his hands in muslin before smoking the bees to create secondary hives. At the first scent of smoke the bees would become disoriented and subdued. I knew the procedure from the habit of watching him and, though he was barely more than a child himself, he was protective and would not let me come too close. That time now seemed once upon a time and worlds away...Now as we talked about the future, he said he would go back to Maputo to look for his mother after Independence. How confident he suddenly seemed, as he confided in me these hopes: candidly, quietly, at the end of the day, when the sun had given the illusion of having set and things appeared to be justly resolved. But of course they would never be justly resolved and even Caetano would disappear from our lives in a manner which I could not at that moment foresee.

10

I WOULD SAY I WAS STUDYING at Andrea's and, after buying chocolate on Rua do Brasil, took the route to the shipwright's factory where Miguel worked. The factory was in an area of the Largo de Camilo Pessanha which was now dangerous, but the only people I saw after school were the old women selling black-market kerosene on the street. His office was up a narrow concrete staircase. Although he had not finished school, he loved to read and there were many books scattered about this small room, along with maps of the world and a few sepia photographs of the Azores which he would seek out in his spare time at the old bookshop in the Rua de Duarte Lopes...His parents, peasants from the Azores, who had dreamed of a better life, were so proud of the son who was now a foreman in the factory which sustained them. But this pride was also the source of Miguel's resentment...His hero was Amílcar Cabral and he had aspirations to study agronomy. He boasted that he wanted to change lives by taking new farming practices to the poor in Africa, in India. The way he talked of these places, it seemed they were distant – rather than an extension of the very earth on which we stood – but I did not say so for fear of treading on his dreams. Some days, I'd find him cheerful when I arrived; on others, pensive – because something had gone wrong at the

factory and the boss had had stern words with him about the
workers whom Miguel regarded as his comrades...Or perhaps
he was morose because he had had an argument that morning
with his father – they were both communists and atheists and
very much alike, but quarrelled all the time. Yet when his mood
lifted, he would say something affectionate, about how his father would monitor the *Journal de Angola* for progress of Salazar's illness, or how much they both liked to eat *kitetas* though
the smell of shellfish drove his mother wild – she prepared
them out of devotion to them both. Some days he would be so
overworked that I would arrive to find him asleep on the old
sofa. I would hesitate to wake him...His face, which I had not
thought so at first, grew more handsome the more I looked at
it; each time I saw it, it was like coming upon a sight in nature
that, existing beneath one's ordinary awareness, suddenly re-
veals all sorts of unspoken truths, an epiphany...Awake, this
face was full of sadness, a *saudade* – a lostness, a feeling of not
having a place in the world. He was very young when his parents had, full of hope and expectation, left Portugal and come
to Angola, yet now they did not know how to return to a life
they had forgotten, to farms that had been abandoned or long
since lain fallow...I would press him to tell me what it was like
on the island. Red of the poppies in April, he would say, and
the sight of the volcano breathing in the distance but as for the
rest, he could barely remember...I enjoyed kissing each part of
him separately. And because of all his preparatory kisses I got
impatient for him to do something momentous, but he would
draw back at this moment and say it was better we waited.
Waited for what, I wondered? He played the guitar like a trou-
badour from Coimbra and also sang English popular songs;

Paul McCartney was a favourite although I contended that it was Lennon who was the real genius. He would open the window and let in the wind off the Atlantic and both this and his voice were a balm. His touch was so tender. Later when I lay on my own small bed at home, I would replay the feeling of his touch in the darkness and this was a vicariousness too. I wondered did he know how to touch me so well because he had touched other women in the same way? I wondered how many girls he had already had, but dared not ask. He knew I was a virgin. Despite his exhortations that we wait, the first time happened unexpectedly and without ceremony. I did not know what I should say. I confessed that it hurt, and cried. He held me, got up and smoked a joint and then played his guitar a little. Then somehow we managed to make love again and I thought, so this is what it is, a sort of closeness but also a being apart: now together, now alone, and also this, being a man, being a woman, forever divided...To improve his English, Miguel was reading *Heart of Darkness*, and he would try out certain phrases on me: 'I flew like mad to get ready, and before forty-eight hours I was crossing the Channel to show myself to my employers, and sign the contract...' Did I know Conrad was writing in a second language and that his real name was Józef Teodor Konrad Korzeniowski? Or that the poet Arthur Rimbaud was a mercenary who had come to Africa and got into the illegal arms trade? I did not know, I told him, for we were still studying Camões at school...Then he shook his head and said how young I was, although the gap was not that great; of course he said it to rile me. Once I opened my Camões and read aloud: 'Love is a fire that burns unseen, a wound that aches yet isn't felt...a longing for nothing but to long, a loneliness in the midst of people, a never feeling pleased when pleased, a passion that gains when lost in thought…', and he snapped it shut and threw the book on the floor. I loved kissing him and could have done only this but soon became emboldened directing his mouth from my mouth to my breasts and then between my legs. Sometimes he would extinguish himself on me and we would simply lie there, spent. I would have to be careful not to fall asleep but often enough this happened, so he'd drop me home on his scooter. My arms sheathed in the warm fleece of his leather jacket, I'd glimpse the smattering of stars amidst the smog…My mother was often already in bed when I got home, reading old *National Geographic*s. She would get up to ask me if I had eaten. As if by habit, she passed me and reached into the pantry for an Alka-Seltzer. Andrea might call. I said nothing of Miguel, although it was as though he was standing there, an invisible presence between us; and I felt my silence, more than any words, to have been the ultimate betrayal. Conversation inevitably turned to our history papers which were due imminently. Our teacher, a young man from Mozambique who was openly a communist, had said history was written from the perspective of the victors, but there were many other, hidden sides…If we looked closely enough, could we not see? Andrea suggested we study at her house together, but the one time I went there, I was unable to concentrate. There was the window, overlooking the manicured garden; the Mercedes, polished and shiny below; the Steinway piano in one corner of the room; the privilege which now made me so uneasy. Andrea was taking copious notes on her chosen topic – the Lisbon Earthquake – and all I could imagine was trembling as Miguel's hands made contact with my body. The topic

I had chosen to write on was an alternative biography of Vasco da Gama and, not knowing where to begin, I had made a column of the navigational feats of da Gama's life culminating in the discovery of the trade route to India; in another column I made an inventory of all the spoils that had resulted from da Gama's first and second voyages – cinnamon, cloves, peppercorns, gold, and, of course, slaves. Then, in another column all the acts of terror and brutality which da Gama meted out to the Muslim pilgrims and traders whom he met with in the Arabian Sea and upon arrival on the coast to the Hindus of Calicut – massacring and burning people alive, cutting off their lips, ears, noses and hands. How ironic, I noted, that this man, who as a small child had wandered among the fisher-folk of Sines, should become Viceroy of India and die in Cochin, another small fishing village, from the bite of an infected mosquito…I was just reading this line aloud to Andrea when Paulo came to the door. I knew that he had had a bitter political argument with Miguel, who had called him a colonial sympathiser and a spoilt petit bourgeois, and now I felt suddenly riven, although I could not have said to what ideology, or whose, I owed my allegiance…One afternoon when I arrived at the factory, Miguel was in a particularly melancholy mood. Amílcar Cabral had been assassinated and the MPLA broadcasts from Brazzaville told of the PIDE's involvement. I asked about the factory, which had run into problems. He said he did not want to talk about it. The factory was to close, he said; the owner had decided to cut his losses and relocate to Lisbon. Now how would he support his parents? By becoming a soldier? He would rather be a mercenary. The family may have to go to Brazil, for there was no farm now to return to in the Azores…

He then spoke of *karma* and fate and said perhaps there were such forces in the world. He said not to get too attached, that nothing could go on forever…I thought I loved him but suddenly realised that this kind of love was a feeling that could pass, perhaps not without pain; that around it there were many lesser and greater worlds, none of them necessarily coincident with the other…I had thought my happiness depended on Miguel, but suddenly saw, with epiphanic clarity, that this was not so. Noise from the street rose up and entered the room: a man shouting 'Elizabeta', then the engine of a scooter. I looked up through the open window and caught sight of the shadows of a couple dancing the *umbigada* with each other, she swaying her hips and encircling him, he clapping to keep the tempo. We lay down and made love. I was suddenly exhausted and soon fell asleep. I dreamt outlandish things, of ships passing through the Arabian Sea, ships heavily laden with stolen and seized treasure, capsizing and spilling their stores of spices and silks and gold. I dreamt of the Lisbon Earthquake, the water bursting the banks of the Tagus and Andrea's Steinway falling through broken flooded floors. When I woke, I told Miguel. He said that I had a vivid imagination and should become a writer. I said that I preferred to live in the world, rather than in words on a page. I preferred to be intimate with things, whereas it seemed a writer had always to be apart, sequestered, even hidden from it, to observe the world so closely. He seemed hurt. How easy it was, I thought, to be close to someone and yet feel out of joint with them and the world…Each time I saw him after that, he was more restless. He kept a set of keys to important parts of the factory on a thick steel chain and often took up these keys from wherever they were, on his desk or hanging from a hook behind the door, and jangled them. One day I arrived and he closed up and we went for a walk around the streets of the Largo do Poeta Bocage: Rua de Antero de Quental, Rua de Almeida Garret and Rua de Fernando Pessoa. At a street stall, we stopped and ate *kifula*. It was then he told me that he was going to Lisbon. He had not told his parents. Eventually Salazar would fall, and he wanted to be there for that; at the first opportunity he would take the entrance exams to enter the University of Lisbon…In the meantime, he would find work on his aunt's farm in the Alentejo. Perhaps I would follow him there? I nodded but in reality could not see myself in Lisbon or the Alentejo or even in the misty Azores. I could not picture myself leaving and starting my sentences on a maudlin note, with a heavy-hearted intonation and the phrase, 'during my time in Africa'. I wanted to cry; I wanted to be stoic and indifferent. A gulf opened up between us, Miguel on one side and me on the other, and it felt vast and deep and unfathomable. We walked back in silence and, when we approached the factory, he asked me if I could come the following day. I did not know if these words made him or me more vulnerable; yet when I saw him with his defences down I was admittedly not moved to comfort him but to beat a hasty retreat. Outside I walked quickly past the women selling kerosene. Some workers were carting packages of cement mix and squatters' children were playing with the split bags that had been abandoned on the jetties. I went to the beach. I liked watching the boys playing football there but they had not come because of the recent police raids. I sat on the rough-hewn stones of the esplanade, devouring a chocolate bar square by square. I stared at the sea. The tide was coming in; a barge was moving along laboriously, its foghorn droning. A child ran with a kite, its elongated shadow flickering on the sand, but hardly did it lift and mount the air before it fell and the string had to be rewound. Insects swarmed around the huge globes of the streetlamps. Two figures, one a man wearing a white suit and a bow tie, the other a woman wearing stilettos, passed me on the esplanade. With each step she wavered like she was high and about to fall. I still had Miguel's jacket on; he had given it to me weeks before and now I took it off, folded it up and left it behind on the old stone parapet. Andrea called when I got home. She had finished her assignment and spoke of her new crush, our history teacher…I was world-weary, my view of love jaundiced, but I maintained my discretion and kept the secret of my own injured pride. I just listened, tears streaming down my face, murmuring some words I'd heard but did not believe, not to get too attached, and nothing goes on forever…

I DID NOT BELIEVE what my mother had said about the dead until I dreamt I saw my father just this way: walking backward, his face to me, his feet headed toward oblivion. There was a wound on his forehead, red and large as a carnation in full bloom. In the dream I wanted to touch this carnation, to carry it off, but my arm, extended outward, could not reach. I cried out and then awoke to find myself in a room not my own, cots configured dormitory-style; crowded, noisy, it was not a place I recognised. It was not a jail – although it may well have been, for there were bars on the windows…At night bats flew in leaving a foetid mess and there were so many mosquitoes I could not sleep for the buzzing at my ears. I had more dreams, nightmares they were…of my mother weeding Papá's grave on the plateau of Rua de São Tomé and waving to me across the tarmac where I was boarding a TAP flight against my will. A well-dressed man with a briefcase took his seat on the other side of me by the window. He did not recognise me but I instantly recognised him as Senhor Mascarenhas…Of a morning, my eyes felt heavy – worlds turned in the time between closing and opening them – and my nightie was saturated with sweat. I would see women wearing white dhotis reapplying disinfectant to the floors, but the smells that returned only hours after, mine no less than any one else's, were invariably human. Apparently, I was in quarantine because of fears that, having come from Africa, I might infect someone with a tropical disease. How did I know this? Like most things about this new country, this terra incognita which I hesitate to call home, it came to me only later, after much bewilderment and angst. Other women moved about me: their *saris* and salwar kameezes rustling, their anklets and bangles tinkling like bells. They gawped and smiled and their presence was at once intimidating and comforting as, assuming I understood, they rapidly fired off conversation in Hindi or Marathi. Out of pity for my incomprehension or my poor appetite or perhaps my being alone, they offered me sweets from their thalis; I took them but they were sickly, saturated with ghee. Eventually I learnt some words – to ask for water, to ask for fruit, to ask what day it was…Time seemed to slow or to have halted. They asked me my name and I lied. Masquerading, I said, My name is Saudade, and, to my surprise, no one unmasked me. I was so lonely yet not at all alone – a paradox I thought of while taking the last of the puris out to feed the birds on the balcony. From here I would watch the huge dusty crows vying for crumbs with the small, undaunted sparrows. A few fair-skinned women were here too; they were hippies, I discerned from their dreadlocks. They kept to themselves and were often to be found asleep in the old, bowed cane chairs or sleepwalking, barefoot, to bum beedis from the wardens. The acrid smoke would drift in with all the other strong smells: frying food, incense and factory emissions – and the alien noises: the call to prayer, a cricket bat thwacking a ball and children running and laughing…Later, when I was let out, I played games of rummy and draughts with a few of these children. They showed me the rules and I observed them closely, like a spy deciphering a code. One girl my age called Mira befriended me; she told me she was coming home from the Gulf where she had been to see her husband. She was so young I did not believe she was already married, but she showed me the proofs by way of her mangalasutra and the intricate but faded designs of the mehndi on her hands. It was only a few days, yet all this came to be routine and those around me almost familiar, when one morning I was summoned to a large administrative outbuilding. My passport, papers and suitcase were summarily given back to me and I was told to get ready: a boat had been booked for me and I would be escorted to the docks by noon…I got dressed, pulling on jeans and a shirt, clothes I had almost forgotten. The streets through the taxi window were thronged with people and slums rose into view at every turn. I arrived at a harbour called Mazagaon, which had once been a fishing village, facing out towards the sea; a sea that, like the last, could disclose so many secrets and so many expectations. Almost as second nature, I knew it was the Arabian Sea and this was Bombay…Near the docks a girl, perhaps half my age, her eyes streaked wildly with *kohl*, tapped my hand and begged for paise. As I fumbled in my pockets, she had me bow my head and draped a garland of marigolds around my neck…On the ferry everyone said I was going home and that it would only be a short journey. Again I had occasion to ponder the meaning of this word, how home may be destroyed by so much strife; how it might be remade from so many makeshift and indiscriminate, even downright unsuitable, materials. I stayed out on deck until the sun had set and the lights off to the south had faded, then retired like everyone else to my cabin. My sleep was light, fitful; my dreams broken but insistent. Outlandish dreams: of whether Andrea's piano would fit up the rickety staircase of her grandmother's flat in the Alfama, whether Miguel's letters to me would come in my absence; whether Caetano would come home…It would be many months before I would learn he had not gone back to Mozambique but died fighting in the civil war…Certain images and words came back to me with a novelistic clarity, but it also seemed like it may all have happened years earlier or to someone else. School closing and coming home to find my mother sitting on the edge of the sofa in her dressing gown, the one with the batik bird of paradise on it, whispering about Caetano's disappearance, the rumours that he had been arrested…Papá also returning early; my mother wringing her hands. For days afterward, his brooding and terrifying presence in the house. The curfew, the blackouts, the rumours of soldiers returning, decamping from their bivouacs on the outskirts of the city…Haze and smoke in the air, the smell of sisal fields burning in the distance. Looking through the window at the empty streets and the neighbourhood curtains drawn. Watching on the television as, overnight, in Largo da República, the Portuguese flag was lowered by the Governor, and another, Angolan, raised by Neto…Papá stalking the corridors, asking not to be disturbed, retiring to his study and, after my mother and I had both gone to bed, the gun shot ringing out, the huge carnation forming…Beads of perspiration glistened on my mother's forehead as she asked me to run and tell the neighbour. Too late, the arrival of the ambulance. In the days afterward, sending me into the newly independent streets with the money for the deposit for the gravestone; the arrangements

for the funeral; frenetic telexes to the Carmelite convent in Goa
and urgent visits to the tourist office to book my ticket and have
my passport prepared. Looking at my father's face in the coffin,
I realised it was a face I had not been able to look at for so long
without being afraid but I did not feel anything other than pity
to see it now. My mother could not look at it and, in the days
after his burial, stared at the garden, meditating on her rotten
lot…On the eve of my departure, I sat on the edge of my bed
for the last time, thumbing through the pages: the photograph
with my hair newly cropped; the date – August 15, 1958 – and
place – Benguela – of my birth; Papá's name and my mother's
maiden name…With the permission it granted me, I was leaving Angola, leaving the continent of Africa perhaps forever.
My passport told a story of where I had come from, but nothing could tell me where I was going; my destiny was unwritten,
a *tabula rasa* all over again. I suppose the beginning always
seems beautiful; we are born unscarred by history's vicissi-
tudes…My mother came to the doorway. I said to her I would
soon be an orphan like Caetano. She said no, it would only be
a short time and we would be together again. In the meantime,
she told me, I would make my home in a village close to the sea
with my grandmother, my father's mother…My mother had
apparently seen to everything. Someone from the village was
waiting at the docks at Navegação to collect me. He put the
luggage in the back of his Ambassador and, as we got into the
car, finger-kissed the picture of São Sebastian that hung from
the mirror. We passed the Summer Palace of Adil Shah; the
Church of Our Lady of the Immaculate Conception, white-
washed, in the baroque style, and the Park of Garcia De Orta.
The Indian flag fluttered and children again played cricket in

the playgrounds, impervious to the archaeologies which surrounded them. We moved along Mahatma Gandhi Road and then turned down longer, more winding roads that led into the villages. Temples rose irrepressibly, to Shiva, to Mahalakshmi and to Shantadurga. I remarked on the red, red earth and the quaint colonial houses and laterite roofs made of this same earth. The vegetation was alien but it was also beautiful – rows of tall coconut and betel groves and undulating paddy fields a lush green I had never seen. Now and again I would sight bougainvillea and moringa, the last my mother's favourite…It was not her house I was going to; rumours had it that it was lying abandoned in another village, the subject of her uncles' ongoing feuds. No, it was my father's house, abandoned also and now, bittersweet legacy, destined to be my mother's as a result of his death. Soon the car turned off a coastal road into a grove of coconuts. Light streamed through the canopy and a dog barked sharply as the car came to a stop. I got out to find myself in another garden – there were large black-and-white butterflies alighting on red hibiscus. The air was humid and the waves of the Arabian Sea crashed in the distance. Perhaps it was where Lord Parashurama had, according to a legend I would be told, created the land, but as I walked forward it was as though I was entering an abyss, and the ground itself was like quicksand. A woman came down from the balcony, redoing the pins in her hair bun. She embraced me and I followed her up into the house. I was told to wash, told to come to table where the old servant, Santana, was laying out lunch. Another stranger, an old man, sat in a wheelchair at the table, gurgling like a baby. I was told he was my grandfather. I now remembered how, in a rare and tender moment, my father had told me that when he was a child he would get into trouble for eating, like Santana, with his hands. He told me he would like nothing other than to get up early in the morning and wait in the kitchen as she heated the leftover kulchi codi so he could mop it up with the freshly baked pão. I began to eat then, with a hunger I had not known, and in just the same manner.

ACKNOWLEDGEMENTS

This work owes much to the encouragement, literary fellowship and support of a number of colleagues and friends. For keeping the faith and for his excellent editorial insight, my sincerest thanks to Ivor Indyk. Thanks to Nick Tapper and Alice Grundy for their careful and sensitive reading. For crucial conversations about the writing in its many stages, gratitude to Kathleen Hill and Darcey Steinke (Sarah Lawrence College), Jennifer Tseng, Peter Bishop, Tif Loehnis, Virginia Peters, Adam Aitken and Roberta Lowing. Thank you to the magical Merrick Fry for nourishing the life of art in many tangible and intangible ways, to Tony Grech for organic affections and my good friend Wanda Greenaway for her loving-kindness. I was fortunate to benefit from a New Work grant from the Australia Council for the Arts and a Fellowship from the Yaddo Corporation, Saratoga Springs, New York, early on in the writing. My thanks also go, last but not least, to my aunt Livia de Abreu Noronha, who lived in Angola with her young family in the period leading up to Independence. In the initial stages of research she gave me a unique sense of place as well as resources that still bear up despite my having been able to find so many of my own errors of fact on Google. Any such inconsistencies, political inaccuracies, or worse infelicities are entirely my own although they issue from the sensibility and poetic licence of a much younger writer.

SUNEETA PERES DA COSTA was born in Sydney, Australia, to parents of Goan origin. Her debut novel, *Homework*, was published internationally by Bloomsbury in 1999. She has published and produced across the genres of fiction, non-fiction, playwriting and poetry and made contributions to Australian literature as an editor, critic and teacher for the Australian Broadcasting Corporation, *Sydney Review of Books*, and the University of Technology, Sydney, among other organisations. Her literary honours include a Fulbright Scholarship, Australia Council for the Arts BR Whiting Residency, Rome, and, recently, an Asialink Arts Creative Exchange to India.

Transit Books is a nonprofit publisher of international and American literature, based in Oakland, California. Founded in 2015, Transit Books is committed to the discovery and promotion of enduring works that carry readers across borders and communities. Visit us online to learn more about our forthcoming titles, events, and opportunities to support our mission.

TRANSITBOOKS.ORG